Blackjack: Driven

By Christopher Ryan

Blackjack created by

Alex Simmons

Published by Simmons & Co. © 2016

CHAPTER 1

Manhattan, August, 1936

Arron Day dropped his bags just inside the door of his luxurious brownstone on the Upper West Side. His servant, Tim Cheng, appeared as he always did, no matter what time Arron arrived, locked up the front and vestibule doors, and then followed Arron as he limped to his bedroom, gingerly stripping the clothes off his wounded and sore body as he went.

"I trust your assignment concluded successfully," Cheng said.

"Tried to kill me," Arron muttered. Each item of clothing was dropped as it came off, which was not his habit.

Cheng dutifully picked them up. "To serve you honestly, Mr. Day, that seems to be part of your particular job."

"My own… my own…"

"Ahh, I see," Cheng spoke calmly even though Arron's words shocked him.

The large, powerfully built man fell into his bed wearing only boxers, bandages, and bruises. He was asleep as soon as he hit the pillow.

"I will make sure you are not disturbed, Mr. Day," Cheng said, lowering the blinds, and closing the curtains to keep the room dark and quiet before exiting, easing the door closed as he did.

Sixteen hours later, a scream jarred him awake from what could have been hours more slumber. "Mr. Day! Run!"

Cheng.

A second protesting yell launched Blackjack out of bed. He landed barefoot on the thick rug, winced as stiff muscles were forced into action.

From the vestibule he heard Cheng in pain. "Let go of my arm!"

Blackjack was across his large apartment in a few quick bounds. He ripped open the front door, recognized Cheng's assailant as Secret Service. Blackjack took one step forward and broke the agent's jaw with a single punch.

As the agent dropped, Blackjack spoke with determined calm, "When I finished my Berlin contract with the US government, I informed your boss Custer that I didn't want to see any of you again. You should have listened." He then addressed Cheng. "I am sorry this man hurt you. Call the police and file a complaint, I will serve as a witness."

Cheng rubbed his shoulder. "What about him?'

"He was endangering you health and safety on private property while trying to gain unlawful entrance into my domicile."

"I understand that part," Cheng said. "I mean about his jaw."

"Suggest to the police that they bring along some medics."

CHAPTER 2

The police were not amused. Detective Fitzpatrick led their arrival. A tough, foul, iron-boned product of the NYPD, Fitzpatrick hated Blackjack the moment they met and had never softened. "Abusing federal agents now, Day? Central booking is going to love this."

Arron suspected Fitzpatrick might show up, and knew if he did, they'd be taking a ride, so he trussed up the agent good and tight, instructed Cheng to watch over him, and then showered and dressed for the occasion. "I was assisting my employee, who was being injured right in front of my door, on my private property, just for doing his job. Add to that attempted forced entrance into my apartment without a warrant and you can see why I concluded that both Cheng and I were in grave danger from some kind of lunatic posing as a law enforcement official."

"That is what happened, detective," Cheng offered.

"Shaddup, coolie," Fitzpatrick barked, and then added, "both of you assume the position!"

Shocked, Cheng turned to his master. "But I did nothing wrong! I do not wish for my family to be deported."

With hands up and against the hall wall and legs spread, Arron was aware of the detective approaching him from behind. He noted twelve ways to dispatch Fitzpatrick from this position, including bringing his left elbow down swiftly to break the foul-mouthed antagonist's neck. Instead, he spoke calmly to his servant. "You are being falsely arrested and I will attest to not only your innocence but your victimization at the hands of this buffoon when I call my lawyer."

"Not from Riker's you won't," Fitzpatrick snarled. He roughly patted down both men, and then yelled at two uniformed cops. "Take them to the paddy wagon and wait for me there."

On their way down the hall, a clearly shaken Cheng looked up at Arron. "What is this Riker's he speaks of? Will it shame my family?"

The much larger man assessed how lost he looked, and knew his man did not recognize the name. "It was built to replace Welfare Island, also known as Blackwell's Penitentiary, which was raided and closed two years ago," Arron explained. When Cheng's face made it clear he was still confused, he added, "It's a prison."

Cheng fainted.

CHAPTER 3

Before the two men could be transported to Riker's, they had to be taken to Central Booking for processing.

"Look at the size of this gorilla," one of the officers said as Arron was brought in.

"We got ourselves an all-day worker here," laughed another. "The judge is gonna wanna put him on a chain gang digging ditches!"

The abuse continued until a phone rang.

One of the louder cops answered, listened, paling visibly, and then pressed the phone to his chest. "Captain, you better take this," he called out.

The shift captain looked out from his office. "Can't handle the phones, McNamara?"

"Not this call, sir."

"Useless mick," the captain yelled, reaching for the phone on his battered metal desk.

McNamara looked at Arron for some reason, perspiration evident on the officer's brow and above his lips, which were moving around without quite forming words.

The processing room at Central Booking grew still as all eyes traveled from McNamara listening in on the call to the Captain and back. Then McNamara flinched, squeezing his eyes closed, and hung up. His face remained scrunched, shoulders crowding his neck as if preparing to be smacked.

The captain walked out silently, approached the still cuffed Arron, stepped behind him, and unlocked the cuffs.

"Take a walk," the captain said, already heading back toward his office.

"Captain," Arron spoke loud enough for all to hear the authority in his voice.

The captain halted, tensed, his face reddening.

"I need Cheng released as well."

Officers gasped.

The captain whirled and marched back. "You think you are in a position to make demands?"

Arron simply extended his arms toward the captain, wrists together.

A vein pounded against the captain's now scarlet neck, threatening its own jailbreak. "You get out of here forthwith or I will re-arrest you!"

Arron raised his arms a bit higher, offering his wrists more obviously.

The captain's eyes darted toward his office as if he could see the source of the call, and then dropped his gaze to the floor, energy draining rapidly. When he raised his eyes it was to glare at Fitzpatrick, "You! Take your weak arrests and get them out of my lock-up before I call your commanding officer and ask at which crap game you won that gold shield!"

The captain stormed into his office, slamming the door so hard it cracked the frosted glass.

The roar from within sounded like someone had just speared a rhino.

CHAPTER 4

The following Friday night, actually early Saturday morning, Arron returned home from a relaxing evening at the Ruby Jean to find his front door ajar. Senses sharpening, Blackjack eased the front door, and then the vestibule open, crept soundlessly across his floor. Silently, he plucked off the wall a set of donga fighting sticks that had been gifted to him by a group of Nguni herdboys in South Africa some years ago, and approached to shadowy living room.

Cheng was bound in a chair, the right side of his face swollen, unconscious. Smith, another of Custer's special agents, sat in Arron's favorite reading chair, a .38 in his hand, a smirk on his face. "Hmmm-mmmm, the late hours you spo--"

One African fighting stick hit him in the throat, Blackjack leaping toward the intruder right behind it, and slamming the other down on Smith's gun hand, shattering fingers.

The smirk was gone.

"After what your team tried, you should be smart enough not to invade my home," Blackjack snarled.

He yanked Smith out of the chair by his gun arm, extended it, and drove his own forearm through the agent's elbow; with a sickening crack, the arm bent the wrong way.

Spinning him around, Blackjack grabbed the other arm, pulled it up and beat the man in the ribs with the remaining donga, clearly hearing three ribs break.

He brought the stick down on the screaming agent's shoulder, hearing a pop there before slamming a foot down on the agent's extended leg, ruining his knee with a loud snap.

The agent dropped into a twisted pile. Blackjack disarmed him, emptying
bullets from his gun before shoving the firearm back into its holster. He grabbed the moaning mess and dragged him to the parquet floor so he wouldn't bleed on the imported rug.

Blackjack dumped the man near his phone, and then untied Cheng, easing him back to consciousness. "Are you able to stand?"

"Do not ... worry about me, Mr. Day," Cheng insisted, every word painful.

"Please call the police again," Blackjack said. "We will need an ambulance this time."

He stood watch over the agent, checking the man's pulse and heart rate to ensure the various breaks were all he'd have to answer for.

CHAPTER 5

Twenty minutes later, he insisted that Cheng allow him to open the door himself. His reasoning became apparent immediately as Detective Fitzpatrick and some uniformed bulls rushed him, pushing Arron inside. Cheng stood by the prone agent, horrified.

"Assaulting federal agents again, Day," Fitzpatrick yelled. "The judge ain't gonna like this."

"Second trespasser in my home," Blackjack said, up against a wall again, this time just an inch away from an actual Fujiwara Kanenga samurai sword presented to him after a successful assignment in Japan.

Fitzpatrick had no clue how close he was to death.

But instead of slicing the detective apart, Arron spoke calmly. "This man broke into my home, assaulted my employee. No telling who he is. I have the right to defend my home."

"He's Secret Service Special Agent Smith," Fitzpatrick announced victoriously.

"Intriguing how you know his name before even checking the man's pockets for identification, detective. I'll note that in the statement I provide my lawyer."

"Don't worry about what I know about him, worry about what I know about you, shine!"

Arron refused to look at the sword, counted to ten.

Cheng spoke up. "Mr. Day's telling the truth, detective. This agent illegally entered--"

"Shaddup, immigrant!"

Cheng's fury was cut short when a voice spoke from the front door. "That will be quite enough of that, detective, unless walking a midnight beat is a career goal for you."

And there he was, Fiorello H. LaGuardia, the beloved Mayor of New York City. Short enough to be called "the Little Flower" he was a commanding enough presence to stop Fitzpatrick in mid-frisk. The detective leapt back from his "suspect" and Arron stepped away from the sword and toward LaGuardia.

"We take home invasion seriously in this city, Mr. Day," the Mayor said, walking right up to Arron with his hand out. "Federal agent or not." LaGuardia shook the dark hunter's hand vigorously.

Detective Fitzpatrick dropped his eyes but couldn't quite shut his mouth. "Special Agent Smith is here on official business, Mr. Mayor."

His honor nodded toward Cheng as his eyes drilled into the detective. "Setting aside this man's clear injuries for just a moment, where's the warrant for entry?" LaGuardia tone was lethal, his authority complete. "Show me paper, now."

The detective searched Smith's pockets, reddening a bit more each time he came up empty. "None, sir."

"Then he's trespassing," LaGuardia said. It was not a suggestion. "Load'em up, and book him at the hospital."

"Sir, he's a Fed--"

"That's an order, detective," LaGuardia said, waving a hand dismissively as he turned his attention to Arron. "Is it possible we might speak privately, Mr. Day?"

Arron stepped into his living room as Cheng held the door for the police. "Please come in Mayor LaGuardia." After the diminutive powerhouse passed him, Cheng glared at Fitzpatrick as he and his bulls carried the broken agent out. Just as the detective was turning to say something, the manservant closed the door on Fitzpatrick's snarling face.

LaGuardia sat in Arron's favorite reading chair. Arron took a seat on the couch. Cheng offered to make coffee or some other refreshment refreshments but the leader of the largest city in the country politely declined. "You look like you've had enough to deal with these past few hours, my friend." Cheng bowed slightly and left them to speak.

Arron was all business. "What can I do for you, Mr. Mayor?"

"After all you've been through recently, it feels like a lot just to ask if you can listen to me for a moment, if you don't mind," LaGuardia answered.

"It would be rude to do otherwise."

LaGuardia laughed. "After all I heard about how you've been treated by government representatives lately, that's pretty rich, you don't mind me saying."

"Honestly, sir," Arron raised and dropped his shoulders as he answered, "My kind gets treated that way regularly. What happened here and overseas was neither surprising nor much different than what millions endure."

LaGuardia looked at Arron. "That bad, huh?"

"Every day, your honor," Arron said, measuring the Mayor's growing unease. Point made, he moved on. "But I suspect race relations is not the reason you are in my home at this late hour."

LaGuardia nodded either in gratitude or acknowledgement of the truth, Arron couldn't tell. Then those powerful eyes locked on his. "I'm here as a favor to the President himself."

"But you aren't even in the same political party."

"I have supported FDR and he's been a big supporter of New York City; both sides have benefitted greatly from our friendship," the Mayor said. "So we keep in touch. When he heard you hospitalized an agent he sent, it was pretty safe to assume his message had not been delivered properly."

"He was abusive from my servant on up."

"And tonight, when President Roosevelt heard about a call coming from your place regarding another injured agent, that's when he called and woke me up, asking that I see you personally to make sure his message finally got to you properly."

"He asked New York City's infamous mayor to see me personally?"

"This is important to him. He heard of your treatment during the Olympics, and about the two agents trying to strong-arm you here. They'll be re-assigned as soon as they are healthy enough to work. Oh, and about you standing your ground with these agents? The President quoted his cousin, 'Bully!'"

Arron gave the slightest hint of a smile.

LaGuardia gave one of his, large and magnetic. "Heh. He told me you don't talk much."

"My contract with the President is completed," Arron redirected the conversation. "What is all this about?"

"Franklin would like it if you would take a private meeting with him, no agents, no problems. Just you and him. At his home, at Springwood, in Hyde Park."

Arron looked at the mayor in silence.

"Look, kid, think what you want. After everything that's happened, who could blame you for being a little short in the trust department? But he's the President of these United States. You gonna turn down the leader of the free world?"

Again, Arron said nothing. LaGuardia left an envelope on the coffee table between them.

"Ya do what ya gotta do, Blackjack, my new friend," the mayor said, patting Arron on the knee before standing. "Good talking to ya."

With that, the most famous mayor in America walked out of Arron's home, tapping the sword on his way out. "Thanks for not using this, kid. You did us all a favor there."

CHAPTER 6

The ride up to Hyde Park offered pretty scenery rather than racist federal agents or overly aggressive police jumping out from the side of the road. As much as he would have preferred to remain tense and annoyed the entire trip, the brilliantly blue sky and multitude of green trees were just too picturesque and Arron found himself relaxing. Maybe this idyllic countryside was why FDR left the White House to come here whenever he could.

But the SS probably don't have a problem with the President's existence, Arron mused, some tension returning.

Hyde Park itself was an appealingly underdeveloped community along the Hudson River about 60 or so miles north of Manhattan. The directions LaGuardia left led Arron to Springwood, an elegant estate set far off the road. He stopped at the gate and reached for the and reached for the handwritten invitation from FDR but was waved in without a word. He drove right up to the classic white columned front entrance and waited, expecting agents to swoop down and demand identification or at least someone to come tell him where to park, but nothing happened.

Not sure why he hadn't been stopped, questioned, or harassed yet (after all, the President of the United States was supposedly here), Arron slowly got out of his car. He stood on the running board and found himself looking around in every direction, searching for charging Secret Service agents.

None emerged.

There were no snipers on the roof.

An armed detail didn't rush him from around the corner of FDR's childhood home.

No shots were fired.

Nothing happened.

And then something did.

An older, serious faced woman saw Arron through a window and hurried to the front door scowling. "Deliveries in the ba--" Her words died when she apparently recognized him. She waddled quickly back into the house without another sound, leaving the door open.

"Okay, what the hell is going on," Blackjack asked no one. He thought for a moment, and then grimaced, "Custer!"

The dark hunter climbed back into his car, put FDR's letter on the dashboard nearest the open driver's side window, the car keys next to it, and placed his hands in plain sight on the steering wheel.

Ten minutes passed.

Blackjack did not move.

Fifteen minutes passed.

Blackjack did not move.

Finally a window was raised on the ground floor to his right. The unmistakable face of President Franklin D. Roosevelt leaned out, cigarette holder held between his smiling teeth. "You are very polite, Mr. Day," he said cheerfully, "but would you do me a favor and come on into my study?"

Arron peered through his windshield at the man, thinking, that's President Franklin Delano Roosevelt. FDR is talking to me.

The voice from above snapped Arron back to attention. "What do you say, Mr. Day? Care for some refreshments and conversation?"

"If you say so, sir," Arron answered.

"That I do," Roosevelt said, his smile widening.

CHAPTER 7

Arron stepped cautiously into the large house. He could feel the presence of people, lots of people, but they were out of sight. What had once been a large living room was now crowded with desks and phone banks and telegraph equipment, all vacant of workers. Arron felt the side of a coffee mug. Still warm.

The Secret Service most probably had men posted along the approach. He had been identified before even entering the property. And everyone had been cleared out.

He couldn't help wondering, what was happening here?

Looking around the classically decorated but now cramped room, Arron caught movement out of the corner of his eye. Through a small opening between two sliding doors, he spied a shadowy figure carrying a body across the adjacent room.

Blackjack charged passed the desks, whipped open the sliding doors – and saw a well-built man placing FDR in a seat behind his desk in front of floor-to-ceiling bookcases. Roosevelt seemed pleased to see him. The man seemed startled and reached for what Blackjack suspected would be a gun.

"Not necessary, this is my guest," FDR assured his aide, patting his forearm until it moved away from his jacket. "I'll be fine. We'll both be, isn't that right, Mr. Day?"

"My apologies, Mr. President," Arron stammered just a touch, "I just saw—it looked like someone had you…."

"Those reflexes of yours are impressive, young man," Roosevelt said, nodding a dismissal to his aide. "Coffee? Something more fun?"

Arron said nothing, trying to read the situation.

FDR smiled, his cigarette holder moving slightly. "Coffee was my mother's idea. I believe I will have an Old Fashioned."

The dark hunter saw that the President had a tray with the cocktail ingredients right on his desk. Without waiting for a reply, FDR started mixing ice cubes, a syrup, a splash of water, some bitters, a generous double shot of bourbon, an orange slice and a maraschino cherry into two glasses. He placed one in front of himself and the other on the far side of the drink tray.

Arron stepped forward and accepted the drink. "Thank you, sir."

"Not at all," FDR waved his hand, either dismissing the gratitude or gesturing for his guest to sit in a chair to the right of his desk. Arron took that seat. FDR raised his glass in toast. "I wanted to thank you for a job well done at the Olympics. I wanted an opportunity to thank you personally as I have discovered not everyone on that assignment understood or appreciated your key role in our success there."

"Wasn't the first time, sir," Arron acknowledged, "And it won't be the last."

"I want you to know directly from me that I neither encouraged nor condoned such behavior," the President seemed chagrinned at the memory. "Your actions were central to the success of our mission in Berlin, and your ability to be discrete at the same time allowed the world to remain focused on the Nazi's failure to defeat the American Spirit so well-embodied by Mr. Owens."

"Had to be done, sir."

The President took a sip and then looked at Arron. "After how you were treated, you still feel that way?"

"What kind of American would I be if I allowed ignorant fools to get in the way of national security, sir?"

"Heroic," FDR repeated, an edge in his voice, "that is what you are. You and Mr. Owens."

"But not heroic enough for you to invite him to the White House with the other Olympic winners."

FDR, shocked, sat back as best he could and seemed to be waiting for an apology.

Arron said nothing.

FDR did the same.

Silence reigned.

Since he was sitting before the leader of the free world, Arron broke the stalemate. "But that is not what you wanted to speak with me about, is it, sir?

"Beyond my apologies for the way things are, son, I am afraid there is a more pressing issue threatening all of our well-being right now."

Again, Arron said nothing.

This time FDR did not wait him out. "You have an unique skill set, Mr. Day, and a hard-won appreciation for the dangers presented by the Nazi Party."

"Are we going to war, sir?"

"I do not see how we can avoid it, but we are nowhere near ready," FDR admitted. "And by saying that, young man, I am trusting you with highly classified information our enemies would kill to possess."

"I am a professional, sir."

"Of that I have no doubt," he said, and then FDR leaned forward, his intensity chilling the room. "In fact, that is why I chose to speak with you and no one else."

"I am going to need an explanation, Mr. President."

"If I could avoid it, we would not be having this conversation, my friend, especially after how things ended in Berlin." The President drained his drink. "But facts are just that; while we are not ready for war, we cannot allow the Nazis to continue their actions in the North."

"North, sir?"

"As in the Arctic Circle, Mr. Day. There is no delicate way to put this; the Nazis plan to melt all of it, and drown their enemies before we are ready to fire a shot."

CHAPTER 8

Arron Day, the international adventurer for hire, was having trouble processing the President's words. "The Nazis want to melt the Arctic Circle, sir?"

"Yes," FDR smiled humorlessly, "they want to melt the Arctic Circle."

Now Arron drained his drink, stood, put it on the tray on FDR's desk. "Is that even possible, sir?"

"Not for us, at least not yet," the President said, hands deftly pouring and adding ingredients for a second batch. "And if our intelligence on how they plan to achieve this is to be believed, their plan lands somewhere between monumentally dangerous and globally fatal."

"Can I ask how, or is that classified?"

"This is need to know, and I believe you need to know," FDR said, handing him a fresh drink. "At the moment, the Nazis are ahead of us in the development of a technology we believe will change the world. How it will change the world is where our opinion differs from theirs."

The president took a sip, nodded his approval, and sipped again before continuing. "Theoretically, we are talking about immense power generated by the scientific splitting of a single atom."

"Pardon my saying so, sir, but that's preposterous."

"Today it is, but both sides are uncovering our future at a rapid pace."

Arron sat back down, stared at his host.

FDR leaned forward once more. "We cannot let the Nazis perfect this technology, let alone use it to flood the coasts of every continent. They will essentially wipe out most of our major cities, as well as those of Britain, France, Spain, Italy, Greece, the African nations, the South American coastline, Japan, and so on. It will cripple any effort to oppose Germany's forces."

Arron's blood ran cold. "Why are you telling me all this?"

FDR leveled a piercing gaze at him. "Because, son, despite the wrongs recently done to you, I am forced to ask you to serve your country once more, and perhaps save the entire world in the process."

CHAPTER 9

The plan was hopelessly flawed and tantamount to suicide.

Immediately after dropping his bombshell, FDR called in generals and colonels from various arms of the military, all of whom smugly argued that their men were better suited than "this one" to carry out the as yet unexplained plan. FDR flatly refused to hear them out. Finally he revealed the reason he was asking Blackjack to brave the Arctic Circle, infiltrate a Nazi base there, and obliterate it without triggering either of the two "negative outcomes" as he put it.

"Which is precisely why we must send in the Marine," a colonial insisted.

"Under no circumstances will we utilize U.S. military forces on this mission," the President insisted. "It must be Blackjack."

So you need someone who is expendable," Blackjack said.

"Untraceable," FDR countered.

Blackjack's smile was mirthless. "Am I not a U.S. citizen?"

The military men made annoyed sounds of dismissal, but FDR silenced them, smiled pleasantly, and leaned toward the adventurer. "You are a citizen I hold in the highest regard, Mr. Day," he assured, "but you offer the additional blessing of having worked in so many parts of the world, in so many nations, for so many different factions of society, both political powers and rebels, as both warrior and liberator, in capacities from personal protection to freedom fighter to treasure hunter, that the Nazis will not be able to categorically prove for whom you are working in the unlikely case that they take you prisoner. In that way, my friend, you are untraceable."

A Naval officer exclaimed, "Our top men can get in and out without fear of capture!"

"Neither our nation nor its military can be connected to this action or we will have launched World War II years before we are ready to participate," the President argued. "That would be devastating for us, for the world … for history."

That was one outcome to avoid, but not the worst. The greater risk was Blackjack causing what the President was terming an "atomic reaction" while executing the destruction of the Nazi base, which would effectively achieve the Nazis' goal of melting the Arctic Circle and drowning most coastlines and major cities.

"Basically, Mr. Day, I am asking you to thread the needle between world war and atomic apocalypse."

"Why not the other guys; the doctor or that mystical gunman?"

"The first is currently missing, reportedly lost at sea; the second cooperates with no one."

"And if I politely decline?"

"According to our best minds, our Plan B increases the likelihood of failure by sixty-five percent. Very possibly, those Nazis you experienced firsthand at the Olympics will rule a smaller, enslaved world."

Blackjack was silent for a long time; the President of the United States and the military representatives waited him out. Finally, the adventurer's steely gaze met the world leader's own warm eyes. "I'm going to have some requests," Blackjack said.

"Of course you are," FDR smiled.

CHAPTER 10

At 3 a.m., Arron paced his brownstone, allegedly packing, but really just unable to sleep. His servant had shuffled drowsily out of his quarters to ask if he needed anything, but Arron sent him back to bed.

But the dark hunter did need something; he needed answers. How was he going to do this? With whom?

It won't be anyone from the government, that much he knew. The truth was he would never completely trust his government again; hand-selected members had demonstrated with almost lethal clarity what they thought of the existence of Blackjack. If FDR hadn't asked him personally, Arron would be sound asleep right now.

That left him the very few people he trusted in the world.

Henri. He had connections to acquire almost anything Arron could think of, and the finesse to use them well. Whether guns or swords or fists, Henri could handle himself well. But he was mostly a strategist, a manipulator of elements, and a daredevil pilot. Arron could use a damn good pilot to cut time on this journey, but even Henri could not fly that far north.

Red and Bo. Comrades in arms. Blackjack trusted these two in any battle he might face, but, if things went even remotely according to plan, this would not be a battle. On this mission, both men would be completely out of their element, and stealth was definitely not Red's strong suit.

Maryam. She was perhaps the most skilled of all of them, maybe even more so than Blackjack himself, but that was in hand-to-hand combat, or on horseback, or wielding knives, swords, handguns, rifles, or even raining machine gun hellfire down from planes. If any of those skills were needed, she was the obvious choice, but not for this. Maryam was a warrior of the desert, not the frozen north.

Arron made a tenth pass through his home, forced himself to acknowledge the truth; he could not justify putting his people at risk on this suicide mission. It would be too long a trip in too cold an environment facing thoroughly one-sided odds outside their skill sets.

Whatever Blackjack was going to do, he would have to do it alone.

CHAPTER 11

The Arctic, October 1936.

Blackjack trained for months with a retired U.S. Marine arctic expert, an Inuk (singular form of Inuit, the indigenous people of the Arctic regions found in Greenland, Canada and Alaska) named Sergeant Thomas Aippaq at the Cape Smythe Whaling and Trading Station near Barrow, Alaska. The training had taken place in the northern most populated area in the United States, 725 miles north of Anchorage, and inside the Arctic Circle. Now he knew a few new things. Chief among them were dogsledding, self-preservation that far north, predators he might come across and how to deal with them, and that he had never been so cold in his life.

Aippaq was much older than Blackjack expected, in his late sixties, but in the impressive physical shape of a man thirty years younger. His gray hair and beard were long ("environmental decision," was all the explanation Aippaq offered), and he was much more Inuit than military in all other aspects as well. Most strikingly, he kept contact with humans to a minimum. For Aippaq, the world revolved around his dogs.

During Blackjack's first day of training, the terse teacher gave his longest speech. "We use Siberian Huskies here because they are faster than Alaskan Malamutes and Eskimo dogs," he said as he presented two dogsled teams, each made up of eight magnificent animals. All sixteen were lean and powerful, predominantly white with some gray or black accents and piercing, ice blue eyes. The few that had tan accents had paler blue eyes. Aippaq's were a shade of blue somewhere in between. All of them, including the teacher, studied Blackjack. "Huskies run with confidence, are sure of foot, determined to serve," Aippaq continued, wading into the sixteen canines crowding around him, touching them with a pat or rub. "Strong, fast, and lightweight compared to other breeds, they can endure this environment and actually love long distant runs. Excellent sled dogs."

He turned, observed Blackjack waiting at the steps holding the metal container he had handed him on their way out to the dog compound. The teacher raised his hands, a question.

Blackjack knew what he was asking. "I am allowing them to smell me, assess my scent."

"Smart man," he said, and then nodded to the container. "An offering to them."

Blackjack opened it, found 16 stripes of beef. He glanced at the dogs, whose heads were raised in anticipation. "Best way to present these?"

Rather than respond to Blackjack, Aippaq addressed the fiercest-looking huskie. "Bob. Go."

Bob strode toward Blackjack. The adventurer glanced at Aippaq, who raised his hand, index and thumb touching, pointing down. Blackjack took a piece of beef and held it out to the dog as the retired marine had demonstrated. Bob padded up to Blackjack, raised its powerful head, politely took the meat into its mouth, and then trotted to the back of the pack.

"Pete."

The next dog did the same.

They did this for all sixteen huskies. When the ritual was complete, Blackjack looked at Aippaq. "Did I pass their test?"

The teacher responded, his back to the dark hunter as he rubbed the dogs some more. "They're not interested in tests; they want to trust you. That you have to earn."

Over several weeks, Blackjack did. The process was slow and deliberate and was incorporated into his education about sledding and survival in the brutal environment where the huskies seemed so comfortable. The education was physical (layers could only do so much), psychological (he had to learn to stop thinking it was cold), and technical (care and feeding of the dogs, driving the sled, learning the terrain).

In addition, he had to acclimate to a very different world than New York City or Europe or the desert or jungle battlegrounds he knew so well. Here snow and ice dominated the landscape as far as the eye could see. Weather-wise, the temperature remained consistently below freezing, with periods of vicious wind and blinding snow, all of it in a perpetual night, which lasted from early October until early March in this region.

More than once, the adventurer wondered whether he would ever acclimate....

CHAPTER 12

The Arctic, December 1936.

It was 3 am, the most northern town in the United States was asleep inside their homes, sheltered from the brutal cold, safe. But for Blackjack and Aippaq, it was time for them, the canines, and two equipment-laden sleds to be loaded onto an Air Force transport that would fly them farther north and over the Atlantic to Greenland, putting them within 100 miles of the target. From there, Aippaq would journey with Blackjack to about two miles from the Nazi base. After that, the dark hunter would be on his own.

They did not have Greenland's permission to be there, but neither did the Nazis.

The journey was long, with one stop on the eastern coast of northern most Canada to refuel and allow the dogs to move for a brief time. Blackjack gazed up at the Aurora Borealis, pretending not to take note of the skeleton crew on duty. Every effort was being made to keep as few people aware of their movements as possible. He appreciated it; surprise would be his only hope for success.

Even with Aippaq and the dogs, ultimately, this mission was about him infiltrating an enemy base and single-handedly taking out the entire facility so definitively even the Nazis would abandon the idea of weaponizing the frozen north for military gain.

However, if one thing went wrong, if he hit the Nazis at the wrong moment, or when their atomic machines were active, then he could very possibly be the one to launch the melting of the polar ice cap, destroying a significant portion of the world, millions of lives (not to mention his own), and most probably hand control of the surviving parts of the planet to Nazis.

He found himself walking a thin line between success and apocalypse, and knew there was no room for error.

Blackjack was racing toward unknown territory to do something he wasn't sure was possible with the fate of the world hanging precariously in the balance.

Bob trotted up to him, placing his head against Blackjack's gloved hand. The adventurer bent down, rubbed the smart dog. "Hey, Bob, how'd we get ourselves into this mess?"

Bob barked.

"Yes, you're right … what do I mean, "we?" Blackjack smiled. "Sorry, fella."

CHAPTER 13

When they finally landed in Greenland, it was on an American-occupied airfield. Blackjack eyed the U.S. military running the landing and unloading their supplies. "How did we manage to acquire this?"

"Money."

After a quick meal and brief time for personal hygiene, the sleds were loaded and secured, and the dogs separated into their teams. Aippaq and Blackjack secured them into their harnesses as the Inuk had taught the adventurer. The older man would work with a team lead by Pete; Blackjack's team leader would be his fierce canine buddy Bob. "He's got your back and has the respect of all fifteen of the others," Aippaq assured. "He'll do most of the driving."

Blackjack nodded, stepped onto the back of his sled as he was taught. It was loaded with food, supplies, and explosives. He made sure everything was secured and then nodded to Aippaq, who had done the same.

With a call of "Hike!" by both men they headed toward an endless, barren night.

The dogs were chosen for their size and strength, but also for their mostly white fur. There would be no spotting these in the distance. Each team of eight worked in perfect unison, charging silently in a synchronized rhythm, becoming nothing more than a blur on the frozen and dark horizon. The white sled, reins, and cargo covering aided in achieving that goal, as did Blackjack and Aippaq's hooded coats, gloves, pants, and boots.

As they drove their packs across the ice and snow, north, always north, he grimaced under his white woolen scarf, eyes blazing behind non-reflective protective glass, only a glimpse of his furrowed brow available.

Memories were granted free reign as they covered the iced over miles.

Blackjack had learned to hate Nazis a few months ago during the summer Olympics in Berlin, during the Jesse Owens mission. That experience made Blackjack vow to throw obstructions in their path himself or via his agents, to send support through trusted channels to finance resistance in key places. But what the President had shown him… the potential of what the Nazis were planning….

That could not stand.

Blackjack would not allow it.

The generals and colonels had given FDR the hard sell, covering his conference table with maps, fuzzy aerial photos, and typed up transcriptions of intercepted Nazi radio correspondence. Even Blackjack's crude understanding of the language was enough to put the pieces together. A platoon, even a strike team, would be detected before they got within twenty clicks of the small science lab up there, the president pressed. After hours of debate and discussions, the generals and colonels were forced to agree.

"This is an unachievable objective," the Marine officer announced.

"Better to risk war by bombing it off the map from the air," the Air Force general insisted.

"I'll go."

"Let's declare war and be done with it," the Army colonel cut in, "why delay the inevitable."

"I said I'll go."

FDR held up a hand. Silence fell on the room, all eyes coming to rest on Blackjack.

The Marine chuckled. "Alone?"

"In specialized gear they will not see me coming."

"I've heard the stories about you," the Army colonel said, shaking his head, "but this is madness."

Blackjack stood up, loomed over the military papers, jabbed a finger onto the pile of pictures and maps. "No, Colonel, this right here is madness." He stood to his full intimidating height and addressed only one person in the room. "I'll leave a list of what I require with your secretary, Mr. President. Including expenses. And triple my usual fee. In advance."

FDR smiled around his cigarette holder, "I like this plan."

Blackjack pulled slightly on the reins, adjusting course. The dogs complied effortlessly.

Got to hand it to the U.S. military, he thought, they spared no expense. Everything he requested, exactly as he requested, including the bank deposit, was fulfilled. Now he was racing across ice and snow trusting dogs to do the rest. He checked a compass periodically, confirming the dogs were exactly on course.

Blackjack almost allowed himself to believe there might be no incident throughout the trip.

Almost.

Before he could complete the leaps in logic it would take to get to that level of confidence, some locals dropped by for a visit....

CHAPTER 14

Aippaq spotted them first, signaled to Blackjack.

Wolves.

The darkness of the night mostly hid them as they approached, allowing them to gain uncomfortable proximity before either man noticed. They ran low, blending with the barren landscape, spread wide to further conceal themselves.

The dogs ran on, a slight change in their body language the only hint that they knew danger lurked nearby.

One appeared on the crest of a low hill, silhouetted in the vague starlight. Her fierce eyes flashed a moment, and then she howled – a rallying cry that dinner had arrived.

The predators crept closer now, still keeping their distance but no longer hiding their presence – another bad sign.

Blackjack could see Aippaq was right; they were wolves. White wolves, to be exact. Indigenous to the Arctic, where the menu was sparse indeed. Maybe some Arctic foxes, Arctic or Snowshoe hares, caribou or reindeer, but none of those had been seen in all the hours they had been travelling. That meant Blackjack, Aippaq, and the dogs were the pack's best shot at eating any time soon.

The wolves must have been starving to even consider approaching men and dog teams. Starvation made creatures desperate, and desperation often proved deadly. And they were surely running desperate now, pacing the sleds easily on either side and behind them. Fleeing this problem was out of the question.

A smart bunch, they kept out of range, barely visible in the dark, just a flash of hungry eyes or gnashing teeth before fading back into the night. But what seemed random revealed itself to be a very clever pattern as the subtle beasts surrounded the sleds more tightly each time they emerged from the murk. Soon all of them were visible, taking up stations three to their right, three to their left, two trotting closely behind.

Eventually one ventured up to the Inuk's sled, testing his resolve to survive. Aippaq answered with a crack of a long whip. Stun across the snout, the wolf galloped away.

The others backed off slightly, but the circle of death remained unbroken and easily kept pace with the sled teams.

Blackjack never mastered the whip so hadn't taken one, and regretted it now.

An older, scarred wolf surprised Blackjack, trotting right up alongside him to his right. The adventurer called out, "Gee!" and the dogs turned right towards Aippaq's team, crowding the damn beast until it dropped back a safe distance.

Aippaq pulled his scarf off, signaled he was about to speak. "They will soon outflank us, will attack in numbers we will not be able to defend against efficiently." he called out. "They are determined to eat."

Blackjack nodded. He counted eight of them now, in loose pairs, at each corner, surrounding the sled teams. There were too many of them, too far from each other for Blackjack to handle by direct confrontation away from the sled.

Two ran up ahead. Blackjack hoped they tried to stop his team; he would drive Bob and the rest right over these cocky hunters, cracking bones before the heavy sled cut up –

That was it!

Blackjack urged the team to his left, Bob resisting several requests, until the adventurer growled, "Haw!"

The dogs grew tense as they went left, reluctantly closing the distance between their safety and the wolves. Blackjack took the reigns with his right hand, slid a long thick knife from his belt with his left, holding it against his gloved wrist and layered forearm and bringing it up against his chest as he watched one of the younger wolves risk galloping up alongside the sled hoping for a taste.

The slash was fast and powerful. It cut deeply. The young wolf fell forward with a confused yelp, rolling over its mostly severed right foreleg, a sudden splash of dark red the only color for miles. An attempt to stand just sprayed more crimson into the gloom, the air taking on a slight hint of copper as Blackjack rode on.

Aippaq's tutelage paid off; the other wolves set upon their wounded brother, ripping him apart in a feeding frenzy, the travellers forgotten amid their bloodlust.

Blackjack matched Aippaq's crack of the reigns and cry of "Hike!" The dogs charged off with renewed vigor, leaving the pack of predators snarling and gnashing in a spreading circle of blood.

CHAPTER 15

Riding putting distance between them and the ravenous wolves, so the men continued an hour beyond midnight. Finally, they slowed the dogs into a small hollow made by winds and an apparently recent upheaval. The hollow offered built up "walls" on the northern and southern sides, which kept the men and dogs out of the strong winds, allowed them to pitch tents that would not be visible from even a short distance, and kept their scent from traveling.

Aippaq believed this last feature to be the most important, "Blood has been spilled. That scent will attract predators from even this distance. As long as the wind is whipping around from the south, even the remains of that wolf will draw hunting animals away from us. Keeping out of the wind makes us virtually undetectable to them for the night – a distinct blessing."

Blackjack got to assembling his tent and feeding the dogs while Aippaq used binoculars to search the horizon for predators. When the adventurer was finished his tasks, he found Aippaq peeking over the low embankment his hand up, signaling silence. Blackjack eased over, raised his eyes above the wall line, and instinctively went for his large knife.

Aippaq whispered, "Nanuk, king of the north."

Not thirty feet away, a polar bear stood, its immense back to them, head held aloft, sniffing the air. The animal was bigger than Blackjack and Aippaq combined, and moved with a muscular grace that only hinted at its power.

A wind rushed at them from the south. The bear seemed to lock in on a scent that interested him and loped away with surprising speed.

Aippaq watched until he was satisfied the beast was focused on something far away, then nodded to his student. "The area should be clear for hours," he said. "Where Nanuk walks, all others flee."

"So we can both get some sleep," Blackjack challenged.

"Winds are fickle," the Inuk shrugged. "A sudden shift could bring our scent right to that one. While his kind rarely attacks humans, he is on the hunt, definitely hungry. I will feel better keeping watch. You have the further trip tomorrow, you sleep."

"I do not expect to get much at all; I am more concerned with getting frostbite laying on this frozen ground."

"The tent is designed to fit little more than you, and the interior is made to keep your body warmth inside," he assured. "You will be surprisingly comfortable."

Aippaq was right, or Blackjack was more exhausted than he thought. Either way, once he crammed himself inside and zippered himself in, the tent warmed with shocking speed.

Five hours later, Blackjack awoke, sensing something was not right. He opened his eyes to find his tent open and Aippaq staring at him, one hand in the big pocket of his jacket.

Blackjack raised one of his huge Colt handguns, aimed it right at the Inuk. "Let's make sure I can see your hands, nice and slow."

Going slowly, Aippaq took his hand out of his pocket, extending it towards the dark hunter. "Beef jerky?"

Blackjack smirked a little bit. "Why the wake up call?"

"Big day," the mentor answered, stepping back so his student could crawl out of the tent and accept the hunk of dried meat. "Best you get an early start."

The adventurer chewed awhile, washing the meat down with swigs from a thermos of now luke warm, very strong coffee. In this environment even tepid liquid warmed him. Through the entire meal, the Inuk studied the adventurer. Finally Blackjack had to ask, "What is on your mind, Aippaq?"

"I have pretty high clearance, I read the file they have on you, I know what they tried in Berlin," he answered.

"Yes?"

The older man's blue eyes shone clear and sharp and openly curious. "You are not in the service; you don't have to take orders from any of them. Why are you up here doing this?"

Blackjack furrowed his eyebrows, grimaced, and then answered, "Because nobody, not federal agents, not FDR, nobody is going to determine who I am and what I do. Except me."

Aippaq just stared at him.

"Those agents from Berlin? The military leaders advising the President? They want us to fail. They need us to fail."

Aippaq interrupted, "No one will ever know what we do here, win or lose."

Blackjack looked out on the seemingly endless gloom of white on white terrain. "Look at us out here, your face and mine the only bits of color far as the eye can see."

"Small specks in a vast wasteland," Aippaq said, shrugging.

"And yet, we're here."

The Inuk looked at the adventurer a long time then gave just a trace of a smile and a single nod. Aippaq handed Blackjack a small sack with the remainder of the beef jerky. "World changer gets extra breakfast."

CHAPTER 16

It was decided that Aippaq and the dogs would stay in the hollow as Blackjack walked the last mile. He strapped snowshoes to his feet, and then loaded up an arsenal of grenade rods (literally grenades with metal rods attached to their bottoms) and secured a rack across his shoulders carrying three M9 rifles. These military issue weapons were capable of firing off a blank cartridge that would launch each grenade rod between 75 and 150 yards, depending on weather conditions.

Blackjack had already donned his equipment belt with the Colts in their holsters at each hip and his large knife sheathed just behind the gun on his right. Having his hood up kept him warm but limited his peripheral vision, and his gloves made for a tight fit of his index finger into his Colts' trigger guards.

If the worst happened, he would have to deal with both before taking action, which would slow him down, but, in this environment, there was no other choice.

The scarf and glasses made conversation impossible, so Blackjack said his goodbyes with a nod to Aippaq and a rub of Bob's neck as he started off, stepping into the windy bitterly freezing night.

Each step made soft sounds *crunch, crunch, crunch* that Blackjack hoped was being swallowed by the wind. Progress was slow, the snow drifts both impeding his tracks and covering them up almost immediately, which would decrease his discovery should the Nazis be crazy enough to send patrols out into this impossible environment.

The plan was simple, walk due north until spotting the base, get close enough to it to effectively destroy the place, walk back, go home. The frigid temperatures and 30 mile per hour winds and drifting snow complicated matters considerably, forcing Blackjack to check his compass often and correct himself when he went even the slightest degree off his chosen path. There was no room for error here in the endless snow and ice; he could get lost forever in this unforgiving world with the merest misstep.

But Blackjack was determined to conquer that, to reach his goals as he had defined them by knowing his terrain and the dangers of the world he was in, and overcoming those obstacles because the world needed him to do this.

Knowing all that did not lessen the wind or heat the air. The terrain remained almost impassible, the environment remained savagely oppressive, and still, Blackjack walked on, one step at a time, his duty on his back, conviction in his heart, and his goal waiting for him up ahead.

Crunch.

Crunch.

Crunch.

CHAPTER 17

After hours of numbing progress, Blackjack finally saw the base emerged from the shadows up ahead. He judged it to be 100 yards ahead, and, walking more softly, he continued on until he was fifty yards from the building. While perfect visibility did not seem possible up here, he saw every marking he was instructed to look for; this was definitely his target.

He would have crept closer, but came across a hollowed out space on a sheet of ice. At first the discovery alarmed him. Clearly this had been dug out; there were even evident scrape marks on the shallow walls. Why would Nazis dig out a space so close to their base?

Sniper nest, he concluded, allowing Nazis to defend against approaching attacks by platoons. He found the reversal amusing as he stepped down into the space and measured the distance to the base from its perfect cover. He was close enough to be both accurate and devastating. He began to unload his weaponry.

Military precision took over as he laid out each rifle, loaded in blanks, and then brought out a grenade rod for each, sliding the rod down the barrel, setting it aside, prepping the next, and then the third. Next he positioned another three blanks and grenade rods for quick reload to finish the job. Finally, he set up a tripod designed to allow him to rest the guns on it, sight the target, fire, and switch weapons quickly.

Everything was ready. The mission was proving smooth, easy even--

Crunch. Crunch.

The sound came from in front of him, above him and about twenty paces away. He was hunkered down in the hollow so he was invisible, or would be until whoever it was checked the sniper's nest.

CRUNCH. CRUNCH.

Louder, and from behind him, to the south, the sound was either closer or much bigger. Had he got himself caught between an armed watch and a returning tank?

Since the northern wall was higher than the southern, and since the dark night would hide him pretty well, Blackjack eased up with his back against the northern side to see what approached from the south.

His spine iced and not because of the weather.

The polar bear was easily ten feet tall. The beast looked every ounce of 700 pounds. The wide claws of her immense paws made it clear that it had been she and not the Nazis who had dug out this shelter. That meant she was pregnant and near to term, and Blackjack was trespassing on territory she would defend savagely.

Suddenly the Nazis were not his main concern.

She was clearly hungry enough to view Blackjack as dinner.

Focused on the death headquarters before him, Blackjack had failed to hear the loping crunch behind him until it was too close.

Crunch.

An immense shadow passed across his face—

The polar bear loomed ten feet from him, rising up, fierce and hungry. She roared. Fierce predatory eyes locked on Blackjack. Powerful forepaws rose, ready to strike—

Out of sheer habit, Blackjack reached for his twin Colts –

Every instinct screamed not to fire those powerful handguns. Shooting this creature might save his life but it would also definitely signal his presence and he'd lose the element of surprise if he had not lost it already to the footsteps approaching from behind the Nazi side of his position. They reportedly had a defense unit there; he did not have the munitions needed for a lengthy battle. He'd be swarmed, overwhelmed, the mission would fail.

Blackjack's hands moved away from the guns, grabbed at his thick knife, not enough but it would have to do. He yanked it from its sheath, calculating attack points – the throat, heart, and arteries. He would have one chance—

The beast rose to its full height, arms extending significantly longer than his own. Blackjack would be unlikely to get in a fatal strike before she slashed him, or slammed him into unconsciousness. He raised the knife anyway as the monster lunged, its immense head snarling, horrible jaws widening as it went in for the kill—

Krakowwww-oww-owwww!

A single shot echoed out across the frozen horizon.

The polar bear's head exploded. The beast fell dead into the crevice beside Blackjack.

That wasn't me, he thought.

From the Nazi side behind him, a voice called out, "Grober Schuss, Franz!"

Another. "Ich war mit dem ziel fur das herz. Ich habe meine trophae ruinert!"

Nazis guards just went hunting, Blackjack thought. And they were approaching to inspect their kill.

Crunch. Crunch. Crunch. Crunch. Crunch. Crunch.

No time to do recon. No telling if there were more than two.

The second voice again, Blackjack noted, grateful they were chatty. "Stan, ich werde zu sehen ob es sealvageable. Wenn dies night der fall ist, lassen sie uns nur lassen sie ihn dort."

A quick look at the nearly headless bear told Blackjack Franz would not be hauling the beast to a taxidermist. The sound of only one set of footsteps continued to advance, giving him the slightest of opportunities.

It's on now. Plans be damned.

His grip tightened on the knife as the steps halted right above him—

"Gott im himmel!"

Blackjack leaped up, slashed the Nazi's calf muscle, stepped to the right as Franz fell, and then stabbed Stan square in the chest. Then he turned, pulling one of the Colts with his free hand, and shot Franz dead. He holstered his weapon, stuck the knife into the low snow wall, and swiftly moved the first grenade rifle into position.

Blackjack secured the tripod, confirmed the steadiness of the mount, sighted the target, needing only a slight adjustment to focus once more on the large double doors –

--which were opening.

He was discovered.

Through the scope, he could see deep within the building all the way to the tank rolling forward to blow him to pieces.

CHAPTER 18

Now or never. Hit the tank. Hope the ordinance inside reacts.

Blackjack fired.

The grenade soared across the fifty hundred yards –

--Blackjack switched rifles, sighting the second as the first grenade reached —

-- the first explosion scattered the emerging foot soldiers as it blazed through the doors, slamming squarely into the tank—

-- the deafening explosion shook the ground, blew holes in the roof—

Blackjack readjusted his sighting to a newly noticed target, fired again.

Some of the foot soldiers had been ripped apart by shrapnel or crushed by chunks of the building. The few rising to their feet could only dive into the snow as the second grenade scorched by them.

This one travelled deeper, igniting a series of explosions that could only mean it hit the fuel tanks powering the place. Brick and mortar and metal and radio towers flew in all directions away lit by the fireball rising from where headquarters had been.

Blackjack's heart leaped. He'd been warned about fire flying into the sky, forming a shape the generals had insisted would rise high into the sky, shaped like a mushroom –

Had he detonated the end of the world?

Blackjack fought for breath as he searched the sky--

The only thing rising into the air was shapeless smoke from the flames.

He picked up the third rifle. Fired again. Reloaded all, fired each into any part of the building still standing until all was wreckage and Nazi death.

Only two soldiers survived, stumbling confused in the flame licked night. Blackjack bent down, relieved Franz of his rifle, and took them out. Mercy killing really; they would freeze in minutes outside without proper gear.

CRUNCH!

CRUNCH!

CRUNCH!

CRUNCH!

Blackjack whirled as another polar bear charged toward the scent of what might possibly have been his mate. The dark hunter had no time to sort out their relationship. The beast was coming, and he dwarfed the female, easily a thousand pounds of outrage. Monstrous, its pure white fur aglow from the distant inferno, a stark contrast to the midnight blue behind it, the sheer size was comparable to the tank Blackjack had just –

Twelve yards away--

He grabbed a rifle.

Ten yards, snarling teeth bared now—

Blackjack scooped up a blank—

Eight yards, a roar welling up in a chest bigger than all of Blackjack—

--the adventurer wrestled the cartridge into the chamber—

Six yards, the roar rumbled the ground—

-- snatched up a grenade rod --

-- Four yards, and up it rose, white, impossible white, blotting out the night, flames flickering it its furious eyes –

-- Blackjack slammed the rifle into his shoulder, aimed—

-- Immense white power was all there was—

-- *Fire!*

Blackjack shot the grenade right into the massive chest—

--The colossus staggered back—

--Blackjack dove away—

--The grenade exploded, ripping the enormous creature apart—

Blackjack rolled away, creating as much distance between himself and the smoldering meat falling to earth as he could. He scramble up and ran. If he became covered in blood, he would attract predators as he walked back.

Once the dark silence reclaimed this barren world, Blackjack examined himself, washing any blood off his clothes with snow, until he was satisfied he'd give off almost no scent.

The remains would attract so much more interest anyway, he acknowledged. There was smoldering meat everywhere.

CHAPTER 19

Blackjack washed and packed the rifles and remaining grenades, and other supplies. After a last look confirmed mission accomplished, he adjusted the equipment he carried, checked his Colts and long knife were in their proper places and easily accessible, and without any fanfare, began the long trek back.

He would find Aippaq, they would toast the moment, maybe even light a cigar, and then begin the long ride back to civilization.

If he was someone else, the right someone else, there would be medals, celebrations, perhaps even a parade.

But that would never happen for either of them. Not in these times.

He would not be returning to report to the President; why give the Secret Service an opportunity to shut him out or worse? Instead, Cheng would deliver a typed report to LaGuardia's office; Blackjack would use FDR's line of communication in reverse. That would be the end of it, no calls to the White House or Springwood. No meetings. He would give none of them an opportunity to diminish what he had accomplished here for himself, for the nation, for the world.

But those who had asked him to do the impossible would know. In their hearts, they would never be able to see the world the same again.

Blackjack knew this, lived with the knowledge of how troubling these facts would be for them, and was glad he had demanded payment in advance.

Blackjack: Red Haze

Written by Alex Simmons

Blackjack created by

Alex Simmons

W hy do we do this? Why do I?

The questions nagged at Arron Day as he walked along a dark and dirty street in a small village in the Northern region of Morocco.

War and poverty had won its battle here. The destitute littered the streets like so many rotting bodies on a battlefield. Just across the Mediterranean Spain was in the throws of a civil war.

France, which consider Morocco a protectorate and was determined to maintain its weakening place in the realm of world powers ... right or wrong.

In Germany, soldiers had just moved into the Rhineland, and a power hungry man named Adolph Hitler was now both Chancellor and President of Germany.

Yes, these were tumultuous times. Greed and hate seemed to spread across the lands like a plague. It was a frightening and changing time for people all over the globe. But for a solider of fortune like Arron Day, Blackjack, the drums of war promised great opportunities.

Arron knew of one other breed that saw gain on the fields of death ... vultures.

As he moved in a steady gait along winding cobble stone streets the question repeated itself. Why had he become a soldier of fortune, a mercenary? Was it truly to follow in his late father's footsteps, or was it for some darker purpose?

And though he was well known, and made a good living at his chosen profession ... instead of spending all his time in beautiful cities, and elegant nightclubs ... the job seem to always bring him to places like this. Or was it the work itself, fighting other people's battles, or protecting them from men as dangerous as himself, which consistently brought him to places where souls died long before their bodies.

The thought lingered in his mind for a moment as he watched a local woman try to pump filthy water from a damaged well in the middle of the street. "Then again," he thought, 'Maybe we didn't create it, but we're certainly not making it any better."

And if that were true, Arron wondered what did the future hold for him?

Up ahead, a glimpse of the run down building squatting at the end of a narrow, dead end street, suggested to Arron this could be the answer to his unspoken question.

The message brought him here was from a fellow adventurer, Russell L.T. Bowman – Bo to those he called friend. His note had been short, but that was no surprise. Like Arron —the expendable men, Bo was often a man of few words.

The building was a derelict two-story structure – a boil on the face of the countryside, which catered to the dregs of the mercenary trade —the expendable men that wander through this corner of Europe.

There were no kerosene lamps hanging by the front door, no candles lit in the grime-covered window. But a half moon gave off enough light to reveal it's pitted walls speckled with cracks, stains and bullet holes. A bit of hemp rope served as a door handle for the wooden door. The large wooden sign above it, made of two long wooden planks, dangled as if at any moment they would drop and bash in the head of anyone foolish enough to pass beneath it. Like the building, the words on the sign had long since faded into near obscurity.

Arron felt the hair on his neck bristle. He knew this was a place men of his world sank into after they'd seen the worse war could offer – seen the wounded, gutted, and dismembered and wanted to forget they'd almost been one of those numbers. Or those who wished they had.

Arron absent-mindedly tapped the twin Walker Colts holstered on his hips, and entered.

The inner chamber was no more than a fifteen-foot square with a narrow, rickety staircase, at one end that led up to the second floor.

Five candles stuck in liquor bottles sputtered around the room casting flickering shadows and giving the place all the warm charm of a musty tomb, or a medieval torture chamber. Foul odors drifted through the air, telling their own stories of the people who lingered here – the drunk, the unwashed, the sick, and somewhere in the walls, the dead.

To his right against one wall someone had created a makeshift bar by laying an old door across two barrels. A little woman stood behind it, as withered and sour as the place itself. She had four dark bottles lined up on the bar. Her expression suggested she'd just as soon spit in your glass and pour you a drink.

Bo was standing tall and straight at the bar. He was a lean, powerful man with a baldpate and reddish brown complexion. "My father was a white missionary, ..." he once told Arron. "... My mother, a full-blooded Cherokee Indian, cast out by her family. So that makes me twice removed. Once from our home, and once from the state."

Bo's grandparents had been among many that the US government had unceremoniously migrated from their homes in Georgia, and the Carolinas, to reservations in Oklahoma. The move had come to be known poetically as the Trail of Tears.

Arron knew all to well, that the loss of dignity and possessions exacted a much higher toll on Bo's people than simply bringing them to tears. During one of their missions in Egypt, Bo had shared the story. "They told my people, you'll have more opportunities," he explained. "They didn't lie. They had more opportunity to be turned down for work and disrespected because they had no jobs. And through the years, it left us with three more opportunities ... to commit crimes and go to prison, to leave, or to drink ourselves into the grave."

Now, watching the Bo stared down at a drink sitting on the counter top in front of him, Arron was still unclear which option the Indian favored.

"I'm here," Arron said flatly as he approached. "Where's Red?"

"Up there," Bo said, nodding towards the stairs.

"Why here?" Arron inquired. "I arrange lodging elsewhere for everyone."

"He couldn't find any place worse." Again Bo glanced at his half filled glass, and then pointed towards the bottle. "Want one?"

Arron shook his head. "How long?"

"Five days."

"You try to –"

"That's not what I do," Bo interrupted. "His choice."

"What do you do?"

"Keep him alive."

"So why contact me?"

Bo chuckled. "You fight evil spirits."

Arron glared at him.

Bo ignored it. "We heard about that job you took on in Scotland," he said. "Figured you could help."

Arron turned to leave. "I'm not a priest."

"He doesn't need a damn priest," Bo insisted. "He needs to talk ... to you."

Arron stopped and turned to face the Indian.

"He don't know it though," Bo continued. "So don't expect a friendly welcome."

"And if I just leave?"

"I figure he'll be dead in two days." Bo finally lifted the glass to his lips and took another sip. "From too much of this ... or somebody's knife." He turned to face Arron. " I know we're not friends. But we fought for you. We fought beside you. That should count for something."

They were a strange pair, Bo and Red. One long, lean, clean-shaven. The other, Red, was more than twice Bo's weight, with long stringy hair and stubbles on his face.

Bo was right, they were not his friends, Arron thought. But he knew they were also more than just hires. The three of them, along with two others had been through a lot. They'd saved each other's lives. In both the Amazon jungles and here on the sands of the Sahara, they'd conquer overwhelming odds. Together they had thwarted Death's efforts to claim them more than once.

That was a bond of a special order. It forged an allegiance that Arron respected almost above all others. And so slowly he turned and walked up the stairs.

There were only two rooms on the second floor. The door to one was open and it was clearly empty, so Arron knocked on the other.

"Go to hell!" A graveled voice shouted from inside. Arron pushed open the door.

The room was narrow – scarcely bigger than a walk in closet. There was just enough space for a single bed in the middle, which ran left to right, leaving just a couple of feet between the end of the bed and a damaged 3-draw dresser. A dingy washbasin sat atop the dresser with an oil lantern next to it casting the only other light in the room.

Red was on the opposite side of the bed, tottering by the soot covered window. He glared at Arron through murky blood-shot eyes. "I didn't tell you to come in," he slurred.

Arron stepped into the room. The air was thick with the odor of human sweat and urine. He saw a bedpan on the floor to his left. Five empty wine and liquor bottles were scatted about the floor, but there was no sign Red had consumed any solid food in days.

The overweight mercenary turned to face Arron. He staggered slightly, his massive 300 plus frame almost missing the wall next to the window. They were only on the second floor, but Arron knew if Red fell he'd certainly break his neck on the hard packed ground below.

"What the hell do you want?" Red growled. He held a bottle in his right hand and Arron could see it was less than half full. "Got no time for you ... big man ... Mr. Day ... Blackjack," he drew out the first half of the word, "... or kin' I just call ya', Massa?"

Arron didn't reply.

Red spit on the floor. "No, no, no ... I got it ... I'll just call ya, Boy."

Arron closed the door, leaned back against it, and folded his arms.

"I didn't say you could stay!" Red shouted. "I'm not working for you right now! Hell, you should be working for me! You should be taking orders from me!"

Red took a long drag from the bottle. "Where I come from, we don't work for no coloreds, no Negroes, no nig –"

Arron's eyes narrowed. "Don't."

"Or what?" Red threw the bottle aside, stepped onto the bed and lunged at Arron. "No one threatens –"

Arron caught the massive fighter by his throat and belt and threw him to the left. Red slammed into the wall and dropped onto the head of the bed causing it to collapse with a loud thud.

"You damn –"

"Again, don't." Arron stepped over to the basin on the dresser. He grabbed up a soiled cloth, dipped it in the brownish water and threw it to Red.

Slowly, Red sat up until he could lean against the wall. He wiped his face with the wet rag, and then clumsily groped among the discarded bottles near him, until he found one that had something floating in the bottom. He patted the bottle, gently, "Old soldier like me ... always something left."

He drained the remnants and then looked up at Arron. "Still here? Like seeing your betters down on the ground?"

"I'm better than you at a lot of things," Arron replied. "So what?"

"So you are looking down on me! I knew it!"

Arron stepped closer to him. "You don't know anything about me. Never did. So, who are we talking about?"

"You, the military, the enemy ..." Red tried to rise to his feet. "Everybody!"

"Who else?"

"I told you."

"No you didn't."

"You deaf?" Red roared. "Every damn son of—"

"Bo?"

"He's a redskin. What does he know?" Red staggered to his feet. "I've saved his hide dozens of times. I saved his life!!!"

This fat, ugly sow from the back hills has kept that baldheaded savage alive and –"

"Why?" Arron asked calmly.

Red stared at him. "Whatcha mean, why?

"Simple question."

"'Cause … 'cause that's what soldiers do … it's what we do."

"It's what friend do."

"I ain't got no friends! Never had! Never!

Red stared at Arron until an evil gleam appeared in his eyes, and a sneer formed across his lips. "Back home in Tennessee we did this here thing," he said and grinned exposing stained teeth. "It was sort of like … sort a like a fox hunt, yeah … Yeah, a fox hunt 'cept with nigras … for sport … fun." Red paused … "What else was there for us ta' do?"

Arron's eyes narrowed. "We never found it sport."

"Well, hounds never consider the feelings of the fox, or coon, now do they?" Once more, Red rummaged through the empty bottles until he found another with something floating along the bottom. "Nope, never did ... and we didn't, neither." His eyes were bleary, yet he seemed to gaze off into some far, murky grey memory.

"We did it lots of times."

Red sat holding the bottle by the neck with both hands, squeezing it so tightly that Arron expected it to shatter in his hands at any moment.

"When you feel that low, you gotta find something lower, got to. 'Else you're thinkin', I'm it! The lowest damn thing on God's green earth!" Suddenly Red slammed one fist against his leg. "And I can't be thinking that! I can't!"

His voice was a hoarse shriek. Spittle flew from his mouth, as he tossed the bottle aside and staggered to his feet. He braced himself against the wall next to Arron.

Arron didn't move. He continued to lean against the door, his arms folded across his chest, his steely gaze locked on the drunken man who whose eyes, though watery, still seem to blaze with hate.

"You know the joke?" Red asked.

Arron didn't respond.

"I didn't need to be stronger than everybody, or even smarter … I just needed to know that I wasn't the only ugly, dirt poor, fatherless fat boy in the county."

"They used ta say, 'Ya momma musta got real friendly with somebody prize hog, Pig Boy!'"

"That's what they called me … every damn day of my life … right up till I run off." Red leaned in closer to Arron, his breath a sickly sour wave of liquor and perhaps the one meal he couldn't keep down.

"Know how I knew I'd done the smart thing?" He swallowed hard… "'Cause when I run off, nobody came lookin' for me … Nobody."

Red's eyes wandered around the room, as if they couldn't fix on any one thing or person. He clenched and unclenched his hands; his breathing was uneven, punctuated by sputters of saliva and phlegm.

He wanted to get to the window, but the bed was in the way. Suddenly he grabbed the thin metal frame, yanked with all his strength, and sent the ratty looking cot flying crashing into the dresser.

Still leaning against the door, Arron glanced from the wreckage to back to Red, who stumbled to the open window. Arron shifted his balance ever so slightly – just in case.

But Red only leaned against the window frame and took a few deep breaths. "Damn close in here. Don't like close. You can guess why." Red stared out into the night.

"So I set out on my own, to see things ... do things. Traveled the rails and the roads, saw a lot of the states ... saw a lot of things ... a lot." Red shuddered as if trying to shake off something crawling across his body.

"Even got close to a little gal back then ... a special one ... till something better came along ... for her. He snickered, "Worked on a freighter and hit a lot of ports, met a lot of people ... nothin' changed. I could see in their eyes, Pig Boy ... So I changed.'

'By the time I reached the West Indies, I was a different man. I was bigger, stronger, and meaner. There was some rebellion going on... Some of the natives didn't like the rulin' powers.

But the sugar crops had to be harvested, so the fightin' had to stop. Some of the whites needed protection, offered better money then the ship. Offered me something else ..."

"A place to put your hate." Arron words were more a statement of fact than a question.

Red half turned toward him and leered. "Yeah. And I had plenty of it. Wasn't long before I was moving up in the ranks. They gave me some men to lead ... locals. Some white, but some were island niggras ... black as tar, fightin' for the boss man."

Arron caught the snide implication, but said nothing. "A couple of'em spoke English. I sure didn't speak their lingo. They knew the enemy, knew the land. I didn't. They kept tryin' to tell me what to do, how to treat the rebels we caught, or the people that hid them."

Red whirled around to face Arron. "Tried to tell me, Tobias Jebediah Janks! Tried to tell a white man what to do!" Red shouted.

"I know what I'm doing, I told them! By then I knew how to cuss' and fight, and kill. I knew it all! I told those black-skinned heathens to shut their face and obey my orders. Obey me! I was in charge! I was finally top dog! And I made'em all jumped to it! Oh, I know they hated me, but they knew their place."

Again, Red paused. He squeezed his eye tight, and pounded his fist against the wall. But whatever he was trying to hold back, would not be denied.

"There was this one group," he said slowly. "This one group of rebels that had been a lot of trouble. They'd come out of the jungles, hit and run, lootin' and all. I wanted them – big bonus if we got'em.

So I gave the order and had my boys locate'em. Had'em scouted out, saw what kind of weapons they had – mostly machetes and a couple of pistols. We had'em out gunned. One of my uppity scouts tried tellin' me my business. Tellin' me ta' wait. I knocked him cold and gave the order and we attacked! We cut right through'em, like a scythe through a wheat field!"

"We destroyed them and we shrieked and cheered, and I could see that big bonus being counted out right into my hands."

Red pressed his head against the wall as tears ran down his cheeks. "The rest' of'em showed up while we were celebratin'. They fell on us like the wrath of God.'

'Now we were out numbered. They had guns, knives, machetes, clubs ... everything they could get their hands on. It wasn't a war, wasn't a battle ... it was a slaughter.

"I was cut and clubbed. They shot me, three or four times. Guess all this fat is good for somethin'." Red chuckled softly.

Arron's voice was quiet, yet firm. "How'd you survive?"

"Luck ... or the man upstairs wanted me to suffer. And I did. They hated me, but they hated the locals more. I laded there among the dead, I was barely breathin', and I could hear the screams as they tortured the ones who fought long side me – 'specially the two that brought us there. The two that had tried to tell me not to attack, tried to tell me what to do ... to warn me.

"They butchered them. Left all of us ... dead men ... laying there and cleared out. We was food for bugs and whatever else came along. Figured I'd feed half the jungle. But some villagers found me. They hid me out, nursed me back to health, kept me alive 'till I could make it back to my boss.'

Know what I found out? My two scouts had come from that village. That's why they knew the area so well. That's why they knew some of the rebels ... They'd all grown up together. And here was their people mending me up after I lead their sons to their deaths."

Red suddenly stood upright. "I said to myself, 'these darkies are fools. They saved the man that got their boys killed!'

Red whirled and smashed his fist through the window. Blood trickled down the back of his hand, but he didn't seem to notice.

"Yeah, I said darkies!" he turned back towards Arron. "Stupid, ignorant niggras, monkeys, and coons!" Reaching into his pocket, Red stumbled toward Arron, "Just like you! They couldn't see I was a killer. They couldn't see that! Can you?"

Without hesitation Red pulled a pearl handled switchblade from his pocket and released the blade as he lunge at Arron.

Arron had earned his reputation as Blackjack. He was fast efficient, and deadly – when he had to be.

Blackjack's right fist slammed into Red's jaw, propelled by the full force of his shoulder and hip as he snapped into the punch. Red's head whipped to the left and his whole body shuddered as the knife dropped from his hand and he fell to the floor.

Slowly, blood dripping from his mouth, Red crawled up onto his hands and knees. He looked up and Arron who stood relaxed before him. He glanced to the Walker Colts in the holsters on Arron's hips. "Why didn't you kill me?"

"If you were still that man," Arron replied, "I would have."

"I got them all killed ... all of'em because I – "

"You want to die, so you can stop thinking about it?" Arron cut him off. "You don't get off that easy. Maybe none of us do. So live with it."

"How!" Red shouted. "How?"

"Do something, or do nothing. Whatever debt you owe, dying isn't the payment. Your punishment is living. What you do with that time is up to you. But don't expect me to lift that weight for you." Arron turned and opened the door. "I've got demons of my own."

Downstairs, Bo was still standing by the bar. The same glass of dark brown liquid was in his hand. It wasn't clear whether or not he'd taken another sip in the time Arron had been gone.

"He still breathin'?" Bo asked nonchalantly.

Arron nodded. "He gets like that a lot?"

"More, since he went back home ... to visit." Bo took a sip. "He tell you the story?"

Again, Arron nodded. "What happened when he went home?"

"He won't say," Bo replied. "He's got a lot of hate in him."

Again Arron nodded. "Why do you ride with him?"

"We all got a lot of hate in us." Bo drained the glass of whisky, placed it on the bar, and studied the half full bottle next to it.

"Why do you travel with him?" Blackjack repeated.

Bo half turned to Arron with an impish grin on his face. "He's a White Eyes. He needs all the help he can get."

Arron returned the grin and walked out into the night.

Once outside, he didn't take notice of the vermin that skittered in the darkness, the smell, or the wanderers that stumbled by. Instead he glanced up at the coal black sky, and the millions of stars made more brilliant by its dark shroud.

He thought about the men he had fought beside and against. About his father who had suffered race hatred, and at times, had heaped it on to others. For a moment, Arron wondered what made him any different from those men, from Red or Bo, or even his closest friend, Henri?

"Why didn't you kill me?" Once more Red's question echoed in his mind. And once again it was followed by the answer he'd not revealed in that room. It was a truth born in something his mother often told him when he was young. When his quick temper often put him and his sister in danger – in a hostile bigoted world.

"To be your own man, you must choose how you face the Devil," his mother would consul. "'Cause sometime he won't send his army against you ... He'll send you a weak sinner, and you'll have to choose whether to offer him a redemption, or death."

Above him the stars twinkled, and the wind rustled the leaves of the trees on the hillside.

Arron suspected he was different, because of his father's skills and his mother's spirit -- maybe because his parents, and sister, had helped him see the value in life, and not death.

Even now, with his parents dead he still had a sister who never let him forget he mattered to her ... that he had family.

Maybe, Arron pondered, a man wants to die because he believes he doesn't matter to anyone and death is all there is.

Arron glanced up to Red's room and the broken window. He thought about Bo, standing vigil in the bar below.

If a man doesn't believe enough in him self, Arron wondered, and if he doesn't have family to keep him sane … can the loyalty of a friend be enough.

It was a question Arron would puzzle on the long walk back to his quarters, and probably for some time to come.

Blackjack is called to a land of bright lights, powerful witches, and cold-blooded murderers. Can even he survive in a world that welcomes every color of the rainbow … except his?

Available on Amazon.com

Twitter: @BlackjackAD   **Facebook**: Blackjack Adventures

www.BlackjackAdventures.com

Made in the USA
Lexington, KY
12 August 2017